The Bath Monster

Colin Boyd

Tony Ross

Andersen Press

After your bath, do you ever wonder
where the dirty water goes?

Jackson loved all the things that
made him dirty and messy.

His favourite thing was to be outside, with his best friend Dexter...

climbing trees...

rolling down hills...

... and playing football.

Every night, Jackson's mother would say,

"Look at you!
Go and have a bath now
or the Bath Monster
will come and get you."

Boys and girls everywhere are told about the Bath Monster and his SECOND favourite food: dirty bath water.

Have you ever spotted the water swirl as it goes down the plughole?

That's the Bath Monster, slurping the dirty water through his special straw.

Every night, Jackson would have a bath,
just to keep the Bath Monster away.

But as he got older, Jackson began to wonder
if there really was a Bath Monster.

One day, when he was out playing football with Dexter, Jackson made an epic save and landed in a big, muddy puddle.

Next, the best friends climbed a tree and Jackson fell into an even bigger, muddier puddle.

Then they ran up the biggest hill they could find, and... that's right, they rolled down it into the **biggest,** squelchiest, **muddiest** puddle EVER!

When Jackson got home, his mother said,

"Look at you!"

"Go and have a bath **now** or the
Bath Monster will come and get **you**."

"NO!" said Jackson.

"I don't believe in bath monsters any more."

The Bath Monster still believed in Jackson though.

That night, he sat under the bath, waiting for his supper of dirty bath water.

He waited, and waited, and waited, and waited, but Jackson did not have a bath.

Now, if the Bath Monster doesn't get any dirty bath **water,** he **must** eat something.

Everybody knows what his SECOND favourite food is, but not many people know what his absolute, tip-top, FIRST favourite food is...

Me?

That night, Jackson found out.